Americans eat nearly 100 tons of sardines every day. They as candy.

Pollen never breaks down. It can last indefinitely.

In Crystal City, Texas, there is a six-foot-tall stone statue of.... POPEYE!

Greyhounds have better eyesight than any other breed of dog.

Welcome to another issue of *Russ Miller's **Oddly Enough**.* I hope you'll find this collection interesting or at least entertaining. For you parents out there that have purchased this book for your children, I hope that you can take a moment to read it with them and help answer any questions that they may have. Do encourage them to run to the Dictionary, or Encyclopedia if they wish to learn more about some of these topics. Pricking the curiosity in the human animal, I believe, is the surest way to develop a true desire to learn. Perhaps something here will be a launching pad for future study.

Indulge me for a moment while I thank those who have meant so much to me in my pilgrimage. First and foremost, I would like to thank my wife of nearly twenty years, Janice Miller. Too, I need to acknowledge my mom and dad, Dorothy and James Robert Miller for buying me books and tolerating my model building and scraps with my sister, Marsha. She's okay too. Finally, thanks to my two kids, Kristin and Erik who have always kept things interesting in my life. I would like to also thank those friends of mine (and they know who they are... though they may not want to be publicly associated with me...) that have encouraged me when I was struggling.

Gary Reed Publisher, James Pruett Managing Editor, Nancy Durand Administrator, Nate Pride Production Manager, Joe Martin Graphics Coordinator, Tim Parsons Projects Editor

ODDLY ENOUGH Published by Caliber Comics 225 North Sheldon, Plymouth, MI 48170. Oddly Enough is ©1997 Russ Miller All Rights Reserved. No part of this publication may be reproduced by any means without the written permission of the publisher. Printed in the USA.

Visit Caliber's Web Site @
www.calibercomics.com

Singer Media Corporation

1030 Calle Cordillera #106 • San Clemente, California 92673 • U.S.A.
PH: (714) 498-7227 • FAX: (714) 498-2162 • E-MAIL: singer@deltanet.com

RUSS MILLER'S ODDLY ENOUGH©

On December 8, 1942, two American pilots sighted a bullet-riddled P-40 with old, outdated markings flying over China from the direction of Japan. A bloody pilot was slumped over the controls and waved slowly at the two fliers. Seconds later, it crashed. Little was found to identify the pilot; however, a diary was discovered in the wreckage. The journal traced the plane back to an island called Mindanao. Somehow, this forgotten American plane, flown by an unknown pilot, found its way across more than 1,000 miles of hostile territory to crash on Allied soil.

ODDLY ENOUGH - The mysterious P-40 had no wheels! This has led many to speculate as to how the machine ever managed to take off at all!

RUSS MILLER'S ODDLY ENOUGH©

Called "the fastest man with a gun who ever lived," Bob Munden of Montana can draw, cock, and fire his single action .45 in a remarkable .0175 of a second. As the world's fastest draw, Munden has won more than 3,500 trophies and hundreds of championships.

ODDLY ENOUGH - Mr. Munden can draw, cock, and fire two shots, hitting two targets so quickly that the human ear can detect only one shot, and the human eye can only see one muzzle flash!

John Wesley Powell taught school in Wisconsin and Illinois until he became a museum curator for the Illinois State History Society. In 1861 he became a volunteer for the Union Army during the American Civil War. He lost his right arm in the battle of Shiloh, but returned to duty a year later to serve with Sherman! He was discharged in 1865. John Wesley Powell in primarily known for being the first man ever to navigate the Colorado River traveling completely through the Grand Canyon. While in the Grand Canyon, John Wesley Powell became trapped on a ledge, where he faced certain death.

ODDLY ENOUGH - His companion, George Bradley, stripped off his own long johns and swung them to Powell, who managed to let go of his grip on the rocky ledge and grab the swinging underwear with one hand to be miraculously pulled to safety!

The French first used pencil sized darts called fléchettes in 1914. These needle sharp darts were carried in canisters slung under the fuselages of airplanes and released from the cockpit.

*ODDLY ENOUGH...*When dropped from an altitude of 1,500 feet, a fléchette could drive completely through the body of a horse!

RUSS MILLER'S ODDLY Enough ©

An outlaw named Big Nose George Parrot lived a mean spirited and unusual life, meeting his end at the hands of a lynch mob that tried several times to hang him from a telegraph pole. The ignorant mob eventually succeeded in allowing George to strangle, hanging from a rope and weighted down by leg irons on March 22, 1881. The undertaker complained that the coffin cover was difficult to nail down because the little man's huge nose interfered with the lid. Later, a Doctor John E. Osborne exhumed the body and tanned the skin of George's chest and thighs to make a medicine bag and shoes. Dr. Osborne also cut the top of his skull off and gave it to his assistant, who filled it with rocks and made it into a doorstop.

ODDLY ENOUGH - During an excavation for a new building in 1950, a whiskey barrel was found that contained the remains of a small adult. The top of his skull was missing. It was the remaining bits and pieces of Big Nose George Parrot!

A horrific accident in September, 1847 changed forever the way scientists thought about brain function. Mr. Phineas P. Gage, twenty five year old foreman, accidentally discharged a powder deposit with a three and a half foot tamping iron. The thirteen pound bar passed through Mr. Gage's head, destroying one eye and displacing a sizable portion of his frontal lobe. Amazingly, Mr. Gage lived through the ordeal, although he was a "different person" from the time of the accident on. He had undergone a type of lobotomy and thus a personality change.

ODDLY ENOUGH - Mr. Gage never lost consciousness throughout the ordeal!

RUSS MILLER'S ODDLY Enough ©

Cody Lundin (Lun-Deen) of Prescott, Arizona (USA) teaches a school in the arts of primitive skills which he calls the ABORIGINAL LIVING SKILLS SCHOOL. During a typical course, students must make their own water carriers from gourds, develop their own fire starting kits, and build their own shelters and process their own meals, all from found plants, animals, and materials in nature. Living a rather Spartan life himself, Cody never wears shoes, even in the snow.

ODDLY ENOUGH - Cody, a white man, has been hired by Indian Tribes to teach these forgotten skills to their children!

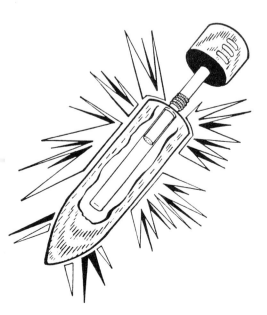

Starting fires from friction "hand drills", "bow drills", or striking flint have been practiced by the human race for tens of thousands of years. One of the most unusual and ingenious of these ancient techniques is a tool called a "fire piston". A tightly fitting plunging rod is slammed quickly into a tube and the heat caused by the compressed air ignites the end of the plunging rod! The same principle as used in Diesel Engines!

ODDLY ENOUGH - These "fire pistons" are still used today in the Philippines as personal cigarette lighters!

THE HOUSE THAT HELL BUILT

Born Herman Webster Mudgett in the 1800's he later became known as "Dr. Harry Howard Holmes" and has the most deplorable legacy of being America's most prolific murderer.

In the beginning, "Holmes" hit on a grisly notion for making money by taking out insurance policies under fraudulent names. Later, he would steal bodies from the dissecting rooms at the University of Michigan (were he was a medical student), disfigure them, plant them at various locations, and collect the insurance money. This scheme worked well until he was discovered by a campus policeman dragging a cadaver out of the lab one evening. It is reported that his response to the cop was "I'm taking my girl for a walk." He was immediately expelled.

"Dr. Harry Holmes" then moved to Chicago where he worked a variety of scams, including buying furniture on credit, selling it immediately for cash and then moving. When he tired of this form of thievery he settled down and got a job as a pharmacist in a drugstore. Because of his stature, rakish good looks, and glib charm, "Dr. Harry Holmes" was able to successfully introduce a variety of "cures" and "health literature" that made him very wealthy. So wealthy in fact that he bought the drugstore.

Across from the drugstore, on Sixty-third street was a vacant lot. "Harry Holmes" bought this property and began building one of the strangest three story buildings ever erected. He kept his horrific plans secret by hiring and firing work crews on a regular basis. The house had turrets, bay windows and several entrances, but, on the inside it concealed trap doors, hidden stair ways, sound proof chambers, dissecting tables, crematories, elevators with no shafts, shafts with no elevators and pits that were later filled with acid and quicklime. "Holmes" passed off his imposing structure as a lodging, and business facility for the upcoming World's Fair of 1893. He told the curious that it was built for tourists and tourist dollars.

While residing at this address, "Dr. Holmes" hired a parade of young secretaries to work for him. After promising to marry them, he would lure them to his ghastly chambers, gas or drug them, and then torture them to death by the most unspeakable means. It is now believed that "Harry Holmes" chopped up and disposed of some 150 persons in this way.

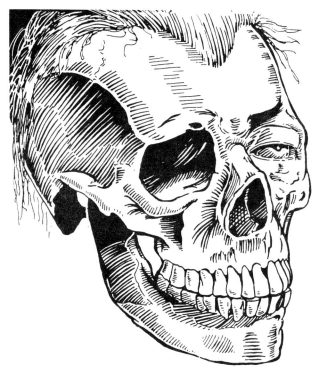

This system of agony and insanity began to unravel when a new love interest refused to sign over her estates to "Harry" when he proposed marriage to her. This particular woman also suspected that "Harry" had other wives and other homes. She shared these beliefs with her sister and her friends. Later she disappeared with her sister, and the rumors began to fly.

In a desperate move for money, "Harry" set fire to a portion of his "Murder Castle" (as it was later referred to by the papers) in order to collect insurance. When inspectors wished to examine his structure on behalf of the insurance company he became indignant and headed for Texas. While in Texas, he worked scams and stole a horse. Caught in a swindle, "Harry" was arrested and later skipped bail. While out on bail he killed again in an effort to remove anyone that had known him or worked with him in the past, including a petty thief.

"Harry" was arrested and sent to Philadelphia to stand trial for murder and fraud. During this time, human remains were found in some houses that "Dr. Holmes" had rented. This led, finally, to an inspection of his huge, meandering Chicago building where the remains of over two hundred corpses were found! Herman Mudgett, alias "Dr. Harry H. Holmes", was tried and hanged in 1896 and was buried (at his own expense) under two feet of concrete in a reinforced coffin!

ODDLY ENOUGH - At the time of his final arrest, Herman Mudgett was served a warrant for horse stealing in Texas. When offered a choice of going to Texas to stand trial, or going to Philadelphia to answer questions about fraud and some disappearances, Mudgett opted for Philadelphia knowing that horse stealing was a hanging offense in Texas!

Nicknamed "Scarface", Al Capone and his gang ran most of the illegal operations in the underworld of Chicago in the 1920s. Throughout his infamous career, Capone and his men killed many rival gang members and were blamed for the famous St. Valentine's Day Massacre. Arrested for income tax evasion, Al Capone spent nearly eight years in prison. He later died in Miami, Florida of syphilis. He had a pathological fear of needles.

ODDLY ENOUGH - Even as one of the richest and most "successful" gangsters of a time, Al Capone was not a made member of the mob (organized crime) because he could not prove his Sicilian ancestry!

In 1878, a retired Union General, Lew Wallace, arrived in New Mexico as governor. Determined to restore order in the feuding Lincoln County Wars, Wallace, in an unusual move, granted amnesty to all outlaws. By corresponding with such "pisteleroes" as the infamous Billy the Kid, he managed to convince many to provide evidence for the State against other wrong-doers. Eventually, his actions helped restore order in the ravaged Lincoln County.

ODDLY ENOUGH - Lew Wallace is *not* known for being a Union General, a Governor, or for his socializing with outlaws. Rather, he is best known for his masterful literary work — *Ben Hur*!

The Coturnix Quail, sometimes called the Pharaoh Quail is the only quail that truly migrates, and when it migrates it moves in huge numbers. A small bird (about 10 to 16 oz.), the Coturnix hens and roosters look very similar with the exception that the rooster carries a bit more russet on his chest and a bit more brown on his head. The eggs that they lay on the ground are effectively camouflaged with speckles that resemble sand, or gravel. The chicks incubate in a remarkable seventeen days and are immediately able to feed by themselves. In Japan, the eggs from these birds are a mainstay and outnumber chicken eggs by a wide margin. One reason for this is that these prolific little animals can lay an egg a day for a couple of years if the feed and conditions are right. When alarmed these birds put their heads down and flare out their feathers that mimic quills, giving the birds a slight hedge-hog appearance. When they roost, they roost in a circle on the ground with their heads facing outward so that if attacked at night they will flush in all directions making it difficult for the predator to pick out one particular animal to feast on.

ODDLY ENOUGH - These are most likely the same quail recorded in Exodus in the Bible. They "covered the camp" and were gathered along with manna by the Israelites for food. Egypt and North Africa are where these animals originated, and to this day they are hunted with sticks because they are so easy to hit out of the air!

The *Sermon on the Mount* preached by Jesus as recorded in the New Testament is actually a prayer of the Essene Jews dating back several hundred years before Christ.

RUSS MILLER'S ODDLY ENOUGH ©

John Paul Jones, the famous American naval hero who uttered the phrase, "I have not yet begun to fight," was born a bastard in Scotland in 1747. He went to sea at age twelve. His real name was John Paul, but he changed it by adding "Jones" after fleeing to America when accused of committing murder. After distinguishing himself during the Revolutionary War, Jones later became a mercenary sailor, becoming involved in piracy and the slave trade. Later in life, he sailed for the Russians and stood trial in St. Petersburg for assaulting a young girl. He died in relative obscurity at age forty-five in France and was buried in an unmarked grave.

ODDLY ENOUGH - In 1905, John Paul Jones' body was brought back to the United States and buried with honors in a tomb at Annapolis!

RUSS MILLER'S ODDLY ENOUGH ©

George "Machine Gun" Kelly, at his wife's urging, built a notorious career robbing banks, kidnapping, and killing those who got in his way. His wife, Kathryn Shannon, used to call the newspapers regularly and brag about her husband and his gang's exploits. George Kelly is credited with coining the expression "G-men" for FBI gangbusters. Even after swearing that "no copper will ever take me alive"--"Machine Gun" Kelly surrendered to the FBI when he and Kathryn were cornered. It is reported that Mrs. Kelly berated her husband for giving up by screaming, "You rat! You've brought disgrace to my family!"

ODDLY ENOUGH - In 1929, although George hated guns, it was his wife Kathryn who bought him a machine gun from a pawn shop and forced him to learn how to use it!

The Kamodo Dragon of Indonesia can measure more than 10 feet in length and weigh a hefty 365 pounds! Its one inch teeth are sheathed in spongy pink gums and are replenished at a rate of 200 per year. An excellent hunter, this beast will eat anything from mice to water buffalo. It has also been known to scavenge when climatic changes pressure it to do so.

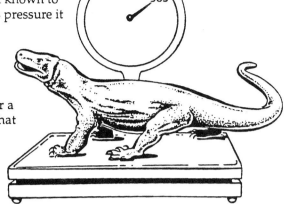

ODDLY ENOUGH... This modern day monster has three eyes! The third eye is located in the top of its head, hidden under a translucent scale. It is believed that this extra eye helps the Kamodo see enemies approaching from behind!

RUSS MILLER'S ODDLY Enough ©

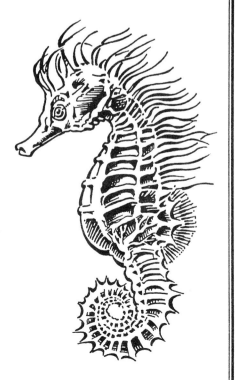

The humble sea horse is actually a member of the pipefish family and can range in size from an inch to one foot in overall body length. They are masters of camouflage, and some sea horses can actually speckle themselves to match bubble patterns in the water. Female sea horses may lay as many as 200 eggs in the male's pouch. When the eggs hatch, it is the male that actually gives birth. Every year millions of sea horses are used in traditional Chinese medicine which has some scientists concerned for the well being of sea horse populations world wide.

ODDLY ENOUGH... Each sea horse has a distinctive crown as individual as a human fingerprint. Some researchers have been able to identify single animals in the wild with no other identifying mark than their heads!

RUSS MILLER'S
ODDLY Enough ©

Dung beetles, sometimes called "Scarabs," roll their eggs into balls of manure and bury them. The ancient Egyptians saw the beetles hatch from soil and revered these insects as symbols of eternal life. So strong was this belief that often Egyptians would remove the heart of the dead and replace it with a Scarab prior to burial.

ODDLY ENOUGH... Some dung beetles mixed clay with the manure, making ceramic-like balls that they buried in large deposits. Some archaeologists, after discovering one of these deposits, mistakenly concluded that they had unearthed an ancient form of cannon ball!

Men occasionally stumble over the truth, but most of them pick themselves up and hurry off as if nothing had happened.
WINSTON CHURCHILL

When you have no basis for an argument, abuse the plaintiff.
CICERO (106-43 B.C.)

When down in the mouth, remember Jonah: he came out all right.
THOMAS ALVA EDISON

And what is a weed? A plant whose virtues have not been discovered.
RALPH WALDO EMERSON

There are more things told than are true, and more things true than are told.
RUDYARD KIPLING

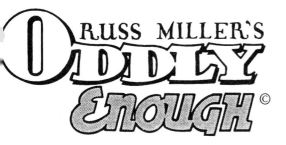

RUSS MILLER'S ODDLY Enough ©

Rumors had circulated for years about a herd of tiny horses trapped in a remote valley of the Grand Canyon in Arizona. In 1938, some Rangers, guided by two Havasupai Indians, did indeed find a band of small horses in the Grand Canyon, but the conclusion that these horses had mutated to this tiny size was a myth. They had, in fact, been descendants of Indian ponies stunted by poor grazing and harsh environment. The shortest horse measured 48 inches at the shoulder.

*ODDLY ENOUGH...*Tiny horses have been exhibited at fairs and sideshows as "Grand Canyon" horses but they were in actuality ponies specially stunted for the purpose of exhibition!

Whenever I hear anyone arguing for slavery, I feel a strong impulse to see it tried on him personally.
ABRAHAM LINCOLN

Who loves not women, wine and song remains a fool his whole life long.
MARTIN LUTHER

I would believe only in a God that knows how to dance.
FRIEDRICH WILHELM NIETZSCHE

Everybody is ignorant, only in different subjects.
WILL ROGERS

RUSS MILLER'S **ODDLY Enough** ©

Humphrey Bogart, winner of a 1951 Academy Award for the movie *The African Queen,* found success in films late in life due to his atypical looks and flinty voice. His partially paralyzed upper lip was due to a wound received in World War I. When Humphrey Bogart died in 1957, he left a legacy of film classics including: *The Maltese Falcon, Casablanca, The Treasure Of Sierra Madre, Key Largo, and The Big Sleep.*

ODDLY ENOUGH...Mr. Bogart's face was in fact well known long before his film career. Humphrey Bogart was the trademark "Baby" on the MELLIN'S BABY FOOD products, and his face (painted by his mother, a commercial illustrator) was seen by millions!

Science deals with unimportant questions that can be solved, while Religion is concerned with important ones that can't.

ARTHUR C. CLARK

God has not given advice from a distance.

DESMOND TUTU
(Nobel Prize Winner)

Bible and science agree that the human species was the last of all living creatures to see daylight on this planet. All other kinds, in the sea, in the air, and on land were here before us. That means that man was the only species absent when the human brain was composed.

THOR HEYERDAHL
(Archeologist, Film maker, Explorer)

RUSS MILLER'S ODDLY ENOUGH ©

Billed as the "Shotgun Wizard," John Satterwhite of West Virginia has out-shot the world six times to capture Olympic Gold Medals for the United States. He currently puts on shooting exhibitions that defy belief as spectators "oooh" and "aaah" at his remarkable prowess.

ODDLY ENOUGH - Satterwhite can hand throw eight clay targets into the air and shoot each before they hit the ground in an astonishing 1.7 seconds!

RUSS MILLER'S ODDLY ENOUGH ©

Alien Hand Syndrome is an unusual phenomena of the human brain. Generally brought on by injury or disease it was first named and recorded by Dr. Goldstein of Germany in 1908. This ailment causes a hand to work independently of its owner's mind. The hand will attempt to prevent the owner from eating, or will close doors immediately after the owner has opened it. The hand behaves unpredictably and often contrary to its owner's wishes. Some victims of this affliction have felt that their hand was demon possessed!

ODDLY ENOUGH - Patients have reported that the hand actually tried to kill them!

RUSS MILLER'S ODDLY ENOUGH ©

Lightning can strike the earth with a force of as great as 100 million volts and is responsible for putting 10 million tons of nitrogen (a critical ingredient for plant growth) into the earth each year. Also, according to Professor Walter Comor of the University of Michigan, men are six times as likely to be struck by lightning as women!

ODDLY ENOUGH ... Oak trees are struck by lightning more often than any other tree! The ancient Greeks considered the oak as a tree sacred to Zeus, the god of thunder and lightning!

Unusual objects have been known to fall from the sky for centuries. These accounts include such bizarre objects as frogs, toads, snails, shellfish, caterpillars, worms, hay, birds, and fish. The largest fish ever recorded as falling from the sky was in India and weighed over six pounds!

ODDLY ENOUGH -
Thousands of snakes fell in Memphis, Tennessee in December of 1876! Even if the reptiles were carried aloft by some freak storm, where such a concentration of animals would have occurred is still a mystery!

RUSS MILLER'S ODDLY ENOUGH ©

Charles Parkhurst, a tough, diligent, stagecoach driver was known for his obsessive concern for keeping stage line time schedules. He once raced a stage across a collapsing bridge rather than go around and deliver his passengers late to their destination. The first time that Charlie was held up by bandits, he quickly shot them both dead. Though a hard drinker, and avid tobacco chewer, Charlie was considered shy and very proper. He was always showing up for work clean shaven. At his death, however, it was revealed that "Charlie" was actually "Charlotte". She had donned men's clothes to escape from an orphanage and had never changed her style!

ODDLY ENOUGH - In 1868, "Charlie" voted in Soquel, California, making her the first woman to vote in a presidential election…years before woman's suffrage created the 19th Amendment allowing women to vote!

RUSS MILLER'S ODDLY ENOUGH ©

Robert Todd Lincoln, son of President Abraham Lincoln, served as Secretary of War under President James Garfield and President Chester A. Arthur. Later in life, he became president of the Pullman Company until 1911. He died in 1926, leaving a legacy of practicing law and statesmanship.

ODDLY ENOUGH - Robert Todd Lincoln was present at three presidential assassinations, President McKinley's, President Garfield's, and his father's!

The sea wasp, or box jellyfish can grow as many as sixty, six foot tentacles and its "hood" can reach the size of a five gallon bucket. It is so transparent that it barely casts a shadow. It is known to eat almost anything, including crustaceans, snails, worms, fish, and one another.

*ODDLY ENOUGH...*This rather unimposing creature is the most poisonous sea animal known to man. It carries three known toxins in it stinging cells including one with enough potency to stop an adults heart in under three minutes!

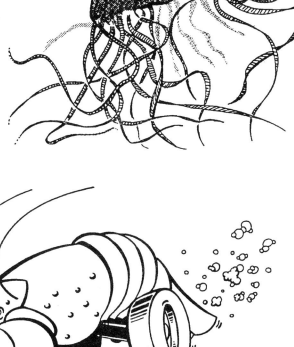

The American Lobster can reach a length of two feet and weigh as much as twenty pounds. Lobsters can be either "right-clawed" or "left-clawed." This interesting sea creature can live for fifteen years, and the females (hens) can lay more than 100,000 eggs at a time. After carrying the eggs around with her for nearly a year, the female shakes them out of the shells and the tiny lobsters rise to the surface until they become large enough to sink to the ocean floor.

ODDLY ENOUGH.... This armor-plated crustacean can move at a rate of 25 feet per second!

RUSS MILLER'S ODDLY ENOUGH ©

In 1929, a new highway was opened between Breener and Bremerhaven, Germany. Within a year, more than 100 autos had mysteriously crashed—all at kilometer stone 239 on a perfectly straight piece of road!

ODDLY ENOUGH - A water diviner, Carl Wehrs, believing the accidents were caused by magnetic force due to an underground stream, buried a copper box filled with copper bits at the base of the highway marker. This was to negate the magnetic force. There have been no further accidents.

RUSS MILLER'S ODDLY ENOUGH ©

In mid-nineteenth century France, a billiard game led to an argument that escalated to a duel. The two men agreed that the appropriate weapon should be a billiard ball!

ODDLY ENOUGH - The first hurler struck his opponent in the forehead-killing him instantly.

I have observed that the world has suffered far less from ignorance than from pretensions to knowledge. It is not skeptics or explorers but fanatics and ideologues who menace decency and progress. No agnostic ever burned anyone at the stake or tortured a pagan, heretic, or an unbeliever.

DANIEL BOORSTIN
(Educator, Social Historian, Librarian of Congress)

Good character is a prerequisite to happiness.
It entails empathy, courage, generosity, work,
honesty, discipline, and balance. It is not easily
achieved. It is not a lesson which can be
learned from books. It requires practice.

JEANE KIRKPATRICK
(Scholar and Public Servant)

...indignation - the cheapest of the emotions-
is righteous for about five minutes. It is the mark
of the sentimentalist that applauds himself when
he only stands and weeps.

JACQUES BARZUM
(Writer, Educator, Scholar)

In ancient Palestine, many of the houses looked something like this, and were made of mud and brick. The roof was usually accessible by a flight of stairs, so that visiting guests could be lodged there Also, because the roofs were made of wood and mud, they had to be repaired periodically after wind and rain storms. For this kind of repair, most households used stone rollers to smooth the patched earthen roof.

ODDLY ENOUGH... Because grass seed often blew onto the roof and took seed, livestock was often allowed up the steps to graze.

What this country needs is a good five-cent nickel.
FRANKLIN P. ADAMS

To abstain from sin when a man cannot sin is to be forsaken by
sin, not to forsake it.
ST. AUGUSTINE

I am dying with the help of too many physicians.
ALEXANDER THE GREAT

When in Turkey, do as the turkeys do.
HONORE DE BALZAC

Every crowd has a silver lining.
P. T. BARNUM

I have seen three emperors in their nakedness, and the sight was
not inspiring.
OTTO VAN BISMARK

Art, like morality, consists in drawing the line somewhere.
GILBERT K. CHESTERTON

I do not paint a portrait to look like the subject, rather does the
person grow to look like his portrait.
SALVADOR DALI

I love fool's experiments; I am always making them.
CHARLES DARWIN

It is much easier to be critical than to be correct.
BENJAMIN DISRAELI

An empty stomach is not a good political advisor.
ALBERT EINSTEIN

Love your enemies, for they tell you your faults. Love your
neighbor, yet don't pull down you hedge.
BENJAMIN FRANKLIN

Pretty much all the honest truth telling there is in the world is done
by children.
OLIVER WENDELL HOLMES

Everything bows to success, even grammar.
VICTOR HUGO

The African Honey-guide is a small, plain looking bird with a rather raspy voice that has been likened to the sound of a matchbox being shaken. Its favorite food is the wax from honeycomb and the bee grubs that live inside. Unfortunately, the bird is so small and thin skinned that it cannot get to the delicious contents of the bee hive by itself.

*ODDLY ENOUGH...*This bird (*Indicator indicator*) has learned to lead more durable animals such as the Honey Badger (*Ratel*) to the beehives, letting them do the destructive work, and giving the Honey-guide access to the comb. African natives have found wild honey by following this little bird for centuries!

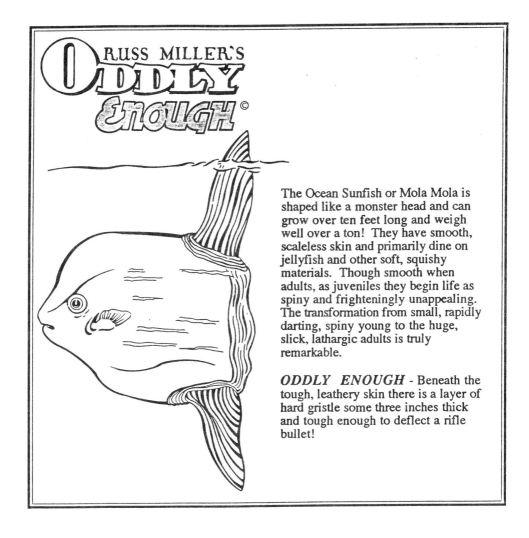

RUSS MILLER'S ODDLY Enough ©

The Ocean Sunfish or Mola Mola is shaped like a monster head and can grow over ten feet long and weigh well over a ton! They have smooth, scaleless skin and primarily dine on jellyfish and other soft, squishy materials. Though smooth when adults, as juveniles they begin life as spiny and frighteningly unappealing. The transformation from small, rapidly darting, spiny young to the huge, slick, lathargic adults is truly remarkable.

ODDLY ENOUGH - Beneath the tough, leathery skin there is a layer of hard gristle some three inches thick and tough enough to deflect a rifle bullet!

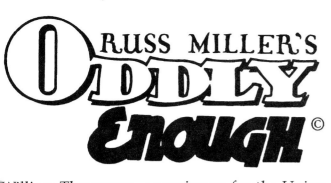

RUSS MILLER'S ODDLY ENOUGH ©

William Thompson, a repairman for the Union Pacific Railroad, was brutally attacked by Cheyenne Indians in 1867 as he worked on a telegraph line. He sustained a tomahawk wound to the head, a gunshot wound to the arm, and had his scalp removed. Leaving Thompson for dead, one of the Indians accidentally dropped the scalp. Struggling for his life, Thompson retrieved his hair, traveled fifteen miles to the nearest railway stations and traveled to Omaha, Nebraska where he asked Dr. Richard Moore to sew the top of his head back on. He had carried the scalp in a bucket of water. Of course, the operation was impossible.

ODDLY ENOUGH - William Thompson's head healed. He later move back to his native England, but first presented his tanned scalp to Dr. Moore as a memento!

RUSS MILLER'S ODDLY ENOUGH ©

The "sweet science" of boxing has been practiced in some form or other for centuries, but the tradition of fixed rules, gloves, and a rope defined ring started in 1743. Gloves became popular after aristocratic boxing fans requested sparring time with the champions of the day. The gloves were referred to as "feather holders" because they softened and lightened the blows to royal facial features. The Marquess of Queensberry rules were composed in 1867 by several individuals, including the Marquess of Queensberry and still stand as the basis for modern boxing regulations.

ODDLY ENOUGH - The longest recorded bout took place in New Orleans in 1893 between Andy Bowen and Jack Burke. It lasted 110 rounds and was declared a draw because after seven hours of fighting, the two boxers were too exhausted to carry on!

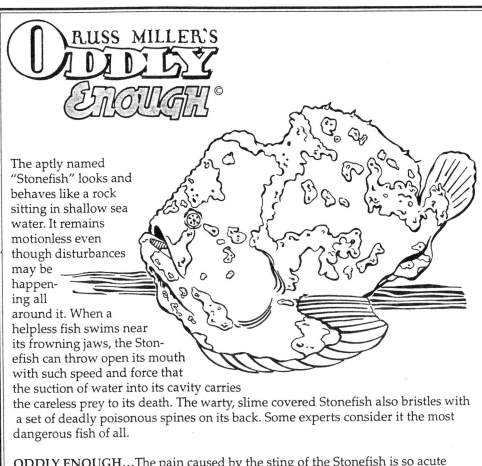

RUSS MILLER'S ODDLY Enough ©

The aptly named "Stonefish" looks and behaves like a rock sitting in shallow sea water. It remains motionless even though disturbances may be happening all around it. When a helpless fish swims near its frowning jaws, the Stonefish can throw open its mouth with such speed and force that the suction of water into its cavity carries the careless prey to its death. The warty, slime covered Stonefish also bristles with a set of deadly poisonous spines on its back. Some experts consider it the most dangerous fish of all.

ODDLY ENOUGH... The pain caused by the sting of the Stonefish is so acute that many people have tried to cut off their own fingers and toes to stop the pain. Others have even tried to kill themselves!

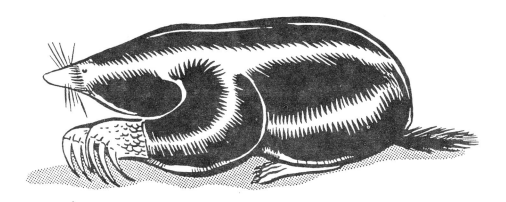

The remarkable little Mole can tunnel as much as 300 feet in one night.

ODDLY ENOUGH ... If deprived of food for as little as ten hours, it will die of starvation!

RUSS MILLER'S ODDLY ENOUGH ©

Benvenuto Cellini, a well known Italian goldsmith from the 1500's was also a gunsmith, marksmen, swordsman, and self-proclaimed adventurer of uncanny luck and ability. Among his best known works is the ten and half foot bronze stature of Perseus. It is rumored that the final model took nine years of work to accomplish.

ODDLY ENOUGH - At the critical moment of pouring the molten metal to cast Perseus, it was discovered that the bronze would not flow properly. A desperate Cellini is purported to have frantically thrown some 200 pieces of his own pewter dinnerware into the cauldron to restore the proper alloy level, and the mold was filled!

RUSS MILLER'S ODDLY ENOUGH ©

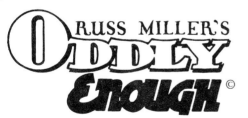

There are many strange stories that involve people being struck by lighting, but one of the oddest concerns an account that took place at Cole Harbor in Halifax, Nova Scotia. A diver working underwater was seriously injured when lightning struck the air pump on the surface to which he was connected!

ODDLY ENOUGH - Though insensible when brought to the surface, the diver survived!

Russ Miller's ODDLY Enough ©

The ruby-throated hummingbird, with its flashy metallic green wings, body, and brilliant red throat has the smallest number of feathers ever counted on any bird. The hummingbird can fly backwards, upside down, and hover, which makes it unique in the bird world. Although tiny, this bird can migrate more than 1,800 miles from the eastern United States to Central America. These hummingbirds build nests of lichen, soft plant leaves, and spider webs. The eggs take only sixteen days to incubate. Because of their small size (1/10 oz.) these birds are preyed upon by frogs, spiders, praying mantises, and even dragon flies!

ODDLY ENOUGH – When the hummingbird feeds on the nectar deep inside a flower, the stamen often touches the bird's head, leaving a deposit of pollen that is carried to the next plant—thus helping cross pollination!

Gold fish will lose their gold color if taken from a pond and put into moving water, such as a stream.

In 1970, a law suit was filed in Arizona against God for allowing lightening to strike a house. The plaintiff won after it was determined that the defendant, God, failed to appear in court.

The plastic or metal tip on a shoelace is called an *aglet*.

The Bay of Fundy, located in Canada between Nova Scotia and New Brunswick can see tidal rises of 60 feet.

Russ Miller's Oddly Enough ©

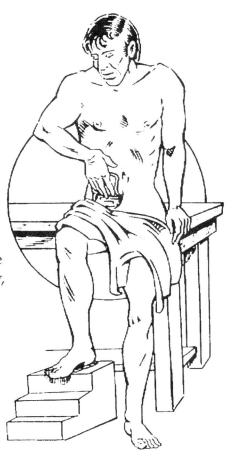

In 1822, a young Canadian trapper named Alexis St. Martin was accidentally shot in the side, leaving a huge gaping wound. An army surgeon by the name of Dr. William Beaumont treated the injured youth and was amazed that the young man lived through the ordeal. Surprisingly, the large hole never entirely healed, and Dr. Beaumont was able to observe first hand how the human digestive system worked. Dr. Beaumont published his findings in 1833, and to this day, 90 percent of his findings are still considered valid.

ODDLY ENOUGH - Alexis St. Martin outlived his doctor by twenty years and was always able to lift a flap of skin to display his working organs.

Russ Miller's Oddly Enough ©

A fifty-six old Spanish thief grabbed the purse of a woman in Alicante, getting in the neighborhood of $170.00. In his haste to escape, he swallowed his own dentures.

ODDLY ENOUGH - The ill-fated man choked to death when the false teeth lodged in his windpipe!

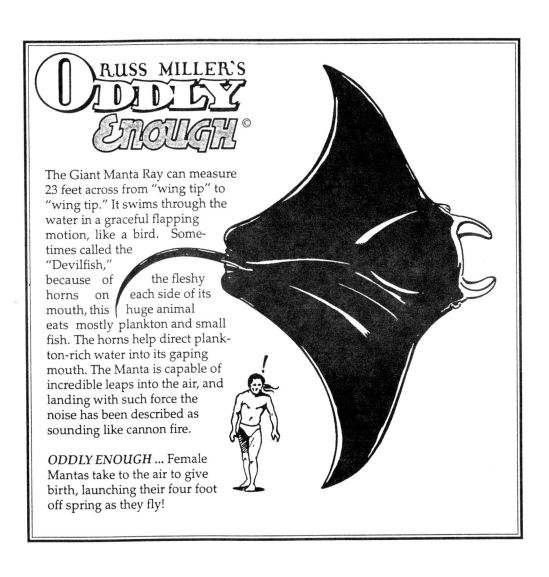

RUSS MILLER'S ODDLY Enough ©

The Giant Manta Ray can measure 23 feet across from "wing tip" to "wing tip." It swims through the water in a graceful flapping motion, like a bird. Sometimes called the "Devilfish," because of the fleshy horns on each side of its mouth, this huge animal eats mostly plankton and small fish. The horns help direct plankton-rich water into its gaping mouth. The Manta is capable of incredible leaps into the air, and landing with such force the noise has been described as sounding like cannon fire.

ODDLY ENOUGH ... Female Mantas take to the air to give birth, launching their four foot off spring as they fly!

The human mouth produces about 2 gallons of saliva a week.

In the early days of surgery, some patients actually exploded on the operating table because the bowels, which contain methane and hydrogen gas were momentarily exposed to static electricity.

The brain of Neanderthal man was larger than our modern brains today.

"Neither snow nor rain nor heat nor gloom of night stays these couriers from the swift completion of their appointed rounds."
Herodotus - Fourth Century B.C.

Sex, age, and race can be determined by scientists from a single hair.

RUSS MILLER'S ODDLY ENOUGH ©

annibalism is not new to the human race. s far back as we have excavated, we ave found traces of people eating eople. In some cultures, cannibalism as brought on by desperation: severe mine, for example. In other cases, it as a sign of domination over eighboring tribes. Cannibalism also erved as a celebration of conquest or art of elaborate religious festivals or hystic rites. Individuals outside of social hores have also been smitten with such hstability that they resort to eating human esh. There is one account of an early Virginia settler (1610) who murdered and ate host of his wife before he was discovered.

DDLY ENOUGH - One of the weirdest accounts of human consumption dates ack to the 1400s in Scotland when a family patriarch and highwayman, Sawney eane, led his family (including grandchildren) on raids from his caves for the pecific purpose of harvesting humans. This tradition went on for years at an stimated one thousand victims!

RUSS MILLER'S ODDLY ENOUGH ©

Early Roman fighting ships carried an array of unique weapons, including folding boarding planks that allowed rapid deployment of troops-two abreast, to board other vessels. Roman admirals also devised ways of using ships lashed together to carry siege weapons, huge catapults, and mounted cavalry.

ODDLY ENOUGH - Roman sailors were also known for throwing jars of live poisonous snakes onto enemy ships when battling in close quarters!

Newts and salamanders have developed some unusual poison defenses in order to protect themselves. Most of the poisonous varieties carry the poison in their skins. This rapidly discourages any would be attacker after the first taste. One California newt also lays eggs that contain a deadly nerve poison, potent enough that one drop would kill thousands of mice.

ODDLY ENOUGH - The Spiny Newt has poison glands at the tips of its ribs. When the little amphibian is squeezed, the pointed ribs burst the glands and squirt poison into the predator's mouth... or an ungloved hand!

The Mantis Shrimp, a reclusive, burrowing sea animal, bears a passing resemblance to the Praying Mantis insect for which it is named. There are more than two hundred types of Mantis Shrimp, ranging from a few inches to more than a foot in length. This creature has the unusual defense mechanism of flicking its "praying" arms forward toward its attacker— or its food victim.

ODDLY ENOUGH ... This flicking action (against water resistance) has been calibrated as matching that of the velocity of a .22 caliber bullet! The Mantis Shrimp has been known to sever a large octopus tentacle with one blow, crush a clam shell, or, while in captivity, to smash the glass of an aquarium tank!

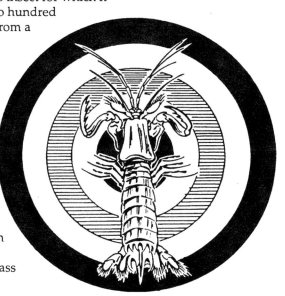

RUSS MILLER'S ODDLY ENOUGH©

Through the ages, beauty has been defined in a myriad of ways depending on culture, ethnic background, tradition, and location. In Sumatra, Indonesia, people file their teeth to sharp points to enhance their looks. In the 1700s, fashionable Japanese women blackened their teeth. Vanity, however, can be lethal. In the eighteenth century in Italy, some 600 men died because their wives put arsenic on their faces to whiten their skin. The husbands kissed them, ingested the poison, and died. Women didn't fare much better after using lead-based white facial make-up that ruined their skin and led to many health problems.

ODDLY ENOUGH - Poppaea Sabina, wife of Roman Emperor Nero, went to great lengths to retain her beauty, including daily baths in asses' milk, covering her face with white lead, coloring her lips and cheeks with *fucus* (a poison), and polishing her teeth with pumice. She even went so far as to paint bluish veins on her bosom to feign youth. Nero had her killed.

RUSS MILLER'S ODDLY ENOUGH©

Smile! False teeth have existed from as early as 700 B.C. but only for vainglorious reasons. The Estrucans and the Phoenicians made wire holders for false teeth, but the functional value of these items was dubious. In the eighteenth century, the insane fad of transplanting teeth from healthy peasants into the mouths of the rich and toothless saw popularity in Europe and America. In some parts of Australia, Aborigines knock out the front two teeth of young men to enhance their looks.

ODDLY ENOUGH - Before the Spanish came to the Americas, the Mayans, Toltecs, and Zapotecs of Central and South America used to drill holes in healthy teeth, and fill the new cavities with gold, turquoise, iron pyrite, and other stones. These inlays were then smoothed and polished!

Spiders have a plethora of traits and specialties. They boast some 30,000 different genera. Some spiders spit venom, some live under water, some throw nets, and others can jump many times their own body length. The largest spider living in South America can grow to the size of a dinner plate, while the smallest, living on the isle of Samoa, is smaller than the period at the end of this sentence.

ODDLY ENOUGH... The Australian Funnel Web Spider, one of the world's deadliest, has fangs so large and strong that it can penetrate bone!

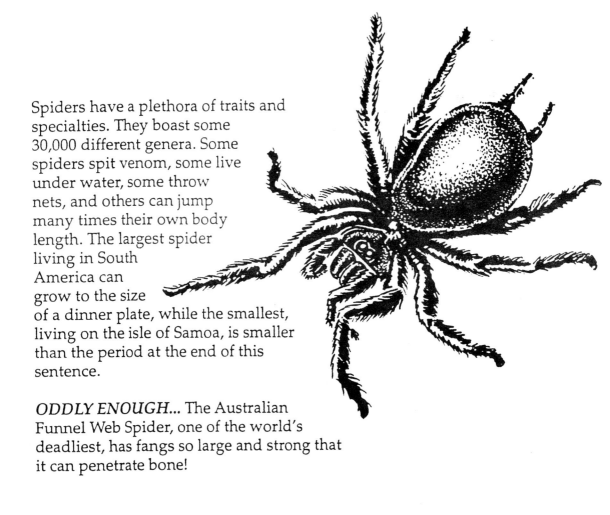

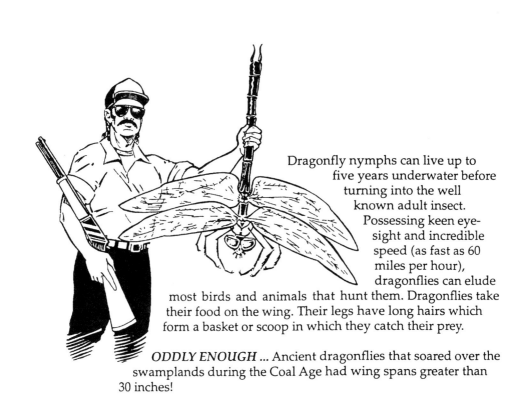

Dragonfly nymphs can live up to five years underwater before turning into the well known adult insect. Possessing keen eyesight and incredible speed (as fast as 60 miles per hour), dragonflies can elude most birds and animals that hunt them. Dragonflies take their food on the wing. Their legs have long hairs which form a basket or scoop in which they catch their prey.

ODDLY ENOUGH ... Ancient dragonflies that soared over the swamplands during the Coal Age had wing spans greater than 30 inches!

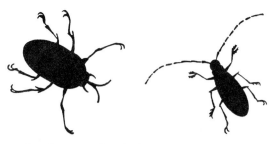

Beetles comprise the largest group of insects on this planet. In fact, for shear diversity and staying power, beetles take the prize. Clearly they represent a fifth of all living organisms and a fourth of all animals living on earth! Their diversity also includes their sources of food. Beetles eat plants, animals, and the remains of both, making them the kings of tiny recycling machines. With a family history of some 230 million years, beetles have proven themselves to have what it takes to survive. Humans have only just begun to scratch the surface of understanding this remarkable little bug.

ODDLY ENOUGH - Some 350,000 species of beetles have been described since 1758! That's an average of more than four new discovered beetles per day!

RUSS MILLER'S ODDLY Enough©

Fungi, like molds, are found everywhere in nature. Whereas, fungus can be used by humans to flavor Roquefort Cheese, it can also be a tremendous nuisance. For instance, fungi, being scavengers, can eat wood, cloth, electrical insulation, leather, food products, ink, glue, paint, sponge, cork, wool, plastics, dead animals, insects, and our food.

ODDLY ENOUGH - The largest single living thing on earth is a fungus, hundreds of years old, found in Washington State (USA) that measures two and a half square miles! It lives about 300 feet underground, and is still growing!

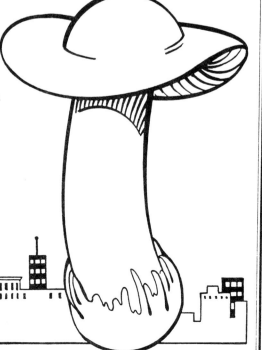

RUSS MILLER'S
ODDLY ENOUGH ©

Susan Winslow, a proprietress of a house of prostitution in Chicago in the 1890s, weighed 450 pounds and was too large for police to take into custody because she could not physically be moved from the premises. After repeated complaints of her illicit operations, officers broke into her place of business and arrested her. Because she would not fit through the door, the frame and walls were sawed away to create an exit.

ODDLY ENOUGH - Susan had be extracted with a horse and dragged to the police station amid her loud complaints about getting splinters.

RUSS MILLER'S
ODDLY ENOUGH ©

The Purity Distilling Corporation owned a huge steel molasses tank in Boston, Massachusetts. The molasses was stored (more than 2 million gallons of it) for making rum. On an unusually warm day on January 15, 1919, the great molasses tank began to burst its rivets, and eventually it collapsed. A wave of black goo more than 30 feet wide swept through the town destroying everything in its path, including an elevated railroad track!

ODDLY ENOUGH - After the ordeal, 50 people had been injured and 21 had been killed! Most of the dead had drowned!

ORUSS MILLER'S ODDLY Enough©

Unlike most owls, the Burrowing Owl of the Southwest United States, prefers living underground in burrows appropriated from badgers, prairie dogs, or ground squirrels. Its habits also differ from other owls in that it remains active around the clock, colonizes in small groups, and has a tendency to behave rather gregariously giving it the nickname of "clown of the plains." Also, instead of hooting, the Burrowing Owl chooses from a repertoire of melodious and soft calls. Its diet consists of beetles, grasshoppers, rodents, scorpions, lizards, toads, snakes, snails, and cacti.

ODDLY ENOUGH...This small bird (9 to 11 inches tall) can and will eat more than its own weight every day!

The smell of a skunk (a member of the weasel family) can be detected by the human nose as far as one mile away. A skunk is capable of accurately spraying (musk) as far as twelve feet away. Its diet consists of eggs, bugs, fruit, grain, and dying or decaying animal flesh. The only known natural enemy of the skunk is the great horned owl, which can swoop down and kill a skunk before it has a chance to react.

ODDLY ENOUGH... The skunk is the only animal known that intentionally eats bees!

There are at least 80 satellites launched from the earth that have broken up into pieces of debris about the size of golf balls. Every year, with every new launch, we unleash more bits of space junk into earth's orbit. It is estimated that there are billions of tiny bits of "space trash" orbiting our planet right now.

ODDLY ENOUGH - The space shuttle received a chipped windshield in 1983 caused by space debris. The replacement windshield cost $50,000. The offending particle of junk was an *orbiting fleck of paint!*

Insects have been prescribed as medicines for centuries. Here are some examples: Ladybugs for colic and measles. Centipedes for jaundice. Wood lice as a laxative.

Active bacteria in a dead body cause gas buildups that can cause the body to swell. Early undertakers found a way around bloated corpses while they awaited burial. By puncturing the body with tiny holes and holding a flame nearby, the gasses would slowly burn off giving the body a bluish glow. Sometimes these strange fires lasted for days.

...trangely literal in their understanding of justice, ...e German and English courts as late as the ...ineteenth century "tailored" punishment to the ...ime.

ODDLY ENOUGH - The wearing of the "Drunkard's cloak" in public included actually wearing a wine or beer barrel in front of the ...cal populace for a designated amount of time!

RUSS MILLER'S ODDLY ENOUGH ©

Nat Love (better known as "Deadwood Dick") was born a slave who was freed after the Civil War and became a cowboy legend. His autobiography chronicles "an unusually adventurous life," including shoot-outs in Mexico, involvement in the Indian wars, and befriending such men as Bat Masterson. When the railroads were well established, and there was no longer a need for the long cattle drives of which Nat had been a foreman many times, he retired from being a cowboy.

ODDLY ENOUGH - Nat Love ended as life as a Pullman porter-the best position open to a black man in those times!

Crocodiles, of which there are twelve known species can grow to more than 12 feet in length and exert more than 1,500 pounds of force between their jaws. They can be cannibalistic, and all swallow their food whole. Crocodiles carry several pounds of stones in their stomach to help grind and digest the large chunks of food they eat. Like the shark, crocodiles continuously grow new sets of teeth to replace those that they lose. Fossils tell us that the ancient crocodiles were as long as 50 feet!

ODDLY ENOUGH - More people are killed in Africa every year by crocodiles than are killed by lions!

Left-handedness tends to be a male characteristic.

Men laugh more than women.

Only female mosquitoes bite and suck blood. Male mosquitoes live on plant juices.

Coffee was once considered an aphrodisiac.

A python can live as long as a year without eating.

THE MAN WHO OUTRAN DEATH

John Colter had already established himself as a tough and durable individual, having survived three years of roughing it in the frontier with the famous Lewis and Clark expedition.

While inspecting beaver traps with another Lewis and Clark veteran, John Potts, the two men found themselves surrounded by members of the Blackfoot Indian tribe. John Potts was killed as he tried to escape. John Colter was captured and turned into a kind of sport by the Indians.

Stripped of all of his clothing, including shoes, John was led to a spot about 400 yards away from a group of armed Indian warriors. At a shouted signal, the Indians began their hunting pursuit of John who miraculously managed to outdistance all but one of the Blackfoot. Realizing that he would not be able to outrun the brave, John turned to fight and managed to kill the Indian with his own spear.

From this point, John Colter made a dash for the Jefferson River where he swam and hid under a pile of floating timbers until nightfall. He drifted down stream for a while in the frigid waters and eventually climbed ashore.

For the next eleven days, traveling day and night, John Colter was completely exposed to the elements. In those eleven days Colter covered an amazing three hundred miles on bare feet until he reached Manuel's Fort on the Big Horn River. He was so battered upon his arrival, he was said to be unrecognizable!

ODDLY ENOUGH - John Colter is also known for being the man who discovered the great thermal springs of Yellowstone National Park!

Of puns it has been said that they who most dislike them are least able to utter them.
EDGAR ALLEN POE

Doctors will have more lives to answer for in the next world than even we generals.
NAPOLEON BONAPARTE

Call no man unhappy until he is married.
SOCRATES

The scallop is a bivalve mollusk and can be found in shallow waters as well as ocean depths of nearly 5 miles. It is the only bivalve with eyes. These bright blue eyes containing the corneas, lenses, and retinas allowing the scallop to see approaching enemies, such as sea stars. The fleshy mantle that contains the eyes is also fringed with numerous tentacles or feelers. The scallop can move by means of jet propulsion when the two shells are snapped together by means of a powerful little muscle.

ODDLY ENOUGH - The scallop can "jet" away with such force that at times it will even break the surface of the water!

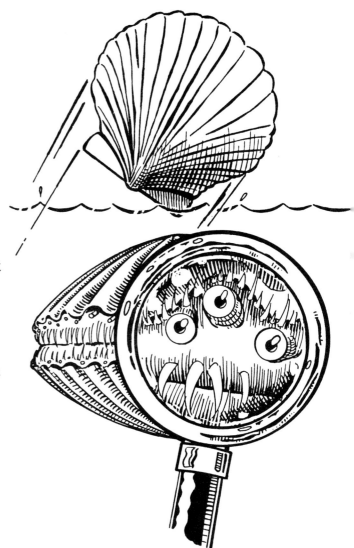

A purple heart was awarded to a jeep in 1943 after the battle of Guadalcanal.

The ant has the largest brain to body size ratio of any animal.

The deer botfly has been clocked at 818 miles per hour.

In the gambling dens of the 18th Century, there were people hired for the sole purpose of eating the dice if the "joint" was raided by police.

The tuna, one of the fastest fish known, can cover 100 miles in a day.

In 1956 a white leghorn chicken laid an egg that weighed more than a pound.

The Great Wall of China is so vast that it can be seen from outer space.

For over 700 years a Greek monastery at Mount Athos has allowed nothing female to enter its area. This includes chickens, horses, and other animals.

RUSS MILLER'S ODDLY ENOUGH ©

After reading Wild West stories and longing for the romance herself, Miss Pearl Hart moved from the East to Globe, Arizona. Miss Hart lived in the Globe area during the 1890's, and was seen carrying rifles and hand guns on her person as a regular part of her daily ensemble. On one occasion, Miss Hart allied with a local drunk to hold up the Globe stagecoach, from which approximately $450.00 was taken from the passengers. After the holdup, while trying to escape, the two bandits got lost and were quickly arrested. Miss Hart received a five year sentence in the Yuma Territorial Prison.

ODDLY ENOUGH - Miss Hart is remembered because she holds the unenviable honor of being the last person to hold up a stagecoach in the United States!

RUSS MILLER'S ODDLY ENOUGH ©

Cowboy movie star Tom Mix, was noted for driving a Rolls Royce car that sported deer antlers on the radiator cap.

ODDLY ENOUGH - Mix once ordered tires for his car with his initials printed on the tread in relief. This was so that when he drove on the many dirt roads in Hollywood, he would have a long rail of imprints (T.M.) in the dust!

The industrious earthworm is as necessary to our existence as the air we breathe. Worms help break down decaying matter in the soil, as well as permit air to enter the ground, thus aiding plant growth. Although worms have no eyes or ears, their skin is sensitive to light, touch, heat, and vibration. Earthworms breathe through their skin, and each worm is equipped as both a male and a female.

ODDLY ENOUGH ... Earthworms range in size from 1/25 of an inch up to 11 feet in length!

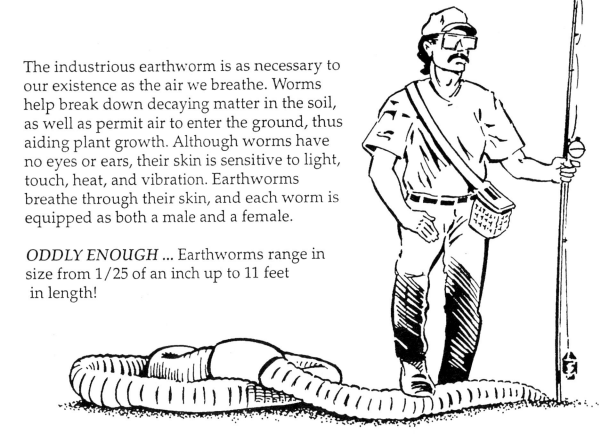

Admiral Horatio Nelson was killed in the Battle of Trafalgar, and his body was shipped back to England for burial. To preserve his remains, he was sealed in a barrel of brandy. When the barrel was opened in England, most of the brandy was gone. Apparently the crew continued to tap the keg. Either they didn't know the whole of its contents, or, they didn't care.

It is reported that the fourth Earl of Salisbury in 1428 was the first man to use cannons in warfare. He also holds the dubious honor of being the first recorded individual to die by cannon.

The only bronze statue that Michelangelo ever finished has never been found. It supposedly was melted down and made into a cannon. Legend has it that the massive cannon exploded the first time it was fired.

There is a statue of a man, dressed in a Roman toga that stands in Pimlico Gardens. He was a popular member of Parliament in his day. His name was William Huskisson. He was the first man to be run over by a railroad train, September 15, 1830.

RUSS MILLER'S
ODDLY ENOUGH ©

he Spanish Inquisition managed to stay financially
ound for so many years due to its high conviction
vel (by the use of torture) and by confiscating the
operty of the condemned "heretics." Eventually, the
nds ran low, and the Inquisition refilled its coffers by
lling position to informers (who also enjoyed
eedom from arrest). By the late eighteenth century,
e Inquisition was essentially broke, although it was
ot truly abolished until 1834.

DDLY ENOUGH - A schoolmaster had the dubious
onor of being the last victim of execution by the
quisition in 1826! He was hanged for heresy because
e had substituted "Praise be to God" in place of "Ave
aria" in his school's prayer!

RUSS MILLER'S
ODDLY ENOUGH ©

The Red Swastika Society of China is a religious order
hat has in its possession some unusual artifacts. One
tem that is referred to as the "sand board" claims to
ontain the "signature of god." On November 21, 1921,
wenty eight devotees of the movement, being directed
hrough the "sand board," scaled the frigid heights of
he "Mountain of a Thousand Buddhas" in Shantung,
China. Their instructions were to set up a camera and take a picture of the sky.

ODDLY ENOUGH - The photograph produced what is revered as "the Picture of
God" and it appears to be an older, dignified Asian gentleman. It hangs over an
ltar in a shrine in Taipei, Taiwan.

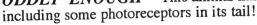

RUSS MILLER'S ODDLY Enough ©

The Horseshoe, or King Crab is not actually a crab at all, rather it is related to spiders. Though primitive looking, it has successfully survived on earth for millions of years. Even though the Horseshoe crab has no natural enemies, it has been exploited by humans for centuries. The tail, or "telson" was used by early people for tips to their fishing spears. These animals have, in recent times, been scooped up from the beaches, when spawning, and used for eel bait, and fertilizer. Now days, the blood of the Horseshoe crab (which is blue due to a copper containing molecule) is used to detect bacterial toxins in drugs and medical equipment!

ODDLY ENOUGH - This animal has no less than ten eyes, including some photoreceptors in its tail!

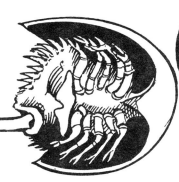

TOP

BOTTOM

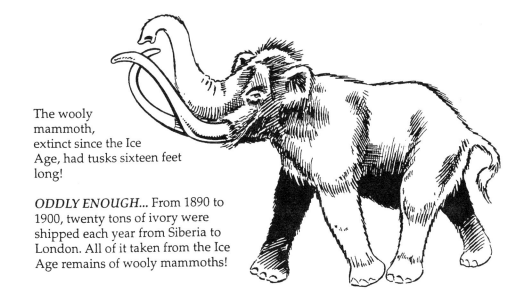

The wooly mammoth, extinct since the Ice Age, had tusks sixteen feet long!

ODDLY ENOUGH... From 1890 to 1900, twenty tons of ivory were shipped each year from Siberia to London. All of it taken from the Ice Age remains of wooly mammoths!

RUSS MILLER'S ODDLY ENOUGH ©

int Ambrose was chose by the people of
ilan to be bishop in 374 A.D. As bishop, he
as advisor to three Roman emperors and helped
efend church freedoms from governmental
terference. It is believed that Saint Ambrose
opularized the practice of singing hymns
church

DDLY ENOUGH - Upon Saint
ugustine's first meeting with Ambrose, he
as struck by the fact that Ambrose read without
oving his lips, a behavior unknown to the
assical world.

RUSS MILLER'S ODDLY ENOUGH ©

n medieval society, criminal punishment for
he aristocrats was considerably different from
hat of peasants. Because of the high cost of
keeping prisoners, only the wealthy were put
nto cells. The poor were usually dealt swifter, cheaper
orrections, which included whipping, amputation, public humiliation, or death.
n one particular ordeal, the prisoner was made to carry a three pound lump of red
hot iron. If his hands had healed in three days when the bandages where removed,
he was considered innocent!

ODDLY ENOUGH - In the seventeenth century, a suspect had to plead "guilty"
before the trial could proceed. Those who refused this plea would be "hard
pressed" with crushing weights until they admitted guilt - or died!

THERE'S GOLD IN THEM HEELS!

Orville Harington, like many others before him, and no doubt others to come, fell under the seductive spell of bright shiny gold. In 1919 he found himself working at the Denver Mint, surrounded by stacks of gold bullion. Having lost a leg due to an accident as a child, Orville felt bitter that he was not being advanced, perhaps because of his affliction. The idea of theft occurred to him, when his artificial leg was replaced by a new hollow, wooden prosthetic limb. The new leg could carry a three pound ingot beautifully.

The Mint knew that gold was being stolen, but there were no suspects. One day, a fellow worker startled Orville when he saw him fondling an ingot. This led a sharp Secret Service officer to plant a small bit of gold near Harington's work bench and then monitor Orville's movements. Sure enough, the gold disappeared at the end of Harington's shift and he was taken into custody. The Treasury found ninety bars hidden in his basement!

ODDLY ENOUGH - Harington said he planned to stop stealing and work for another year before he would go out and buy an abandoned mine. There, he planned to take his ill gotten gold, melt it down, and sprinkle it into the tunnels where he could conveniently strike it rich!

SOUR CHERRIES

The Celebrated Cherry Sisters have been billed as the World's Worst Entertainers. They began their so - called careers in 1893 and apparently were so bad that they became successful simply because people loved to hurl abuse and projectiles at them while they played. After the Des Moines *LEADER* published an unflattering article regarding their act the sisters sued the paper.

The court ordered the Cherry Sisters to perform before the judge. The *LEADER* won. To this day most legal textbooks cite the Cherry Sisters' case on First Amendment rights, Freedom of Speech.

ODDLY ENOUGH - When the Cherry Sister act opened on Broadway in 1896, a barrier of net was erected across the stage in order to protect them from thrown objects!

Probably the cheapest .45 caliber pistol ever built was this "Liberator" manufactured by General Motors and Guide Lamp Co. in 1942. Over one million were made at a cost of $1.71 each and were designed to be distributed throughout Europe to those people sympathetic to America and her allies.

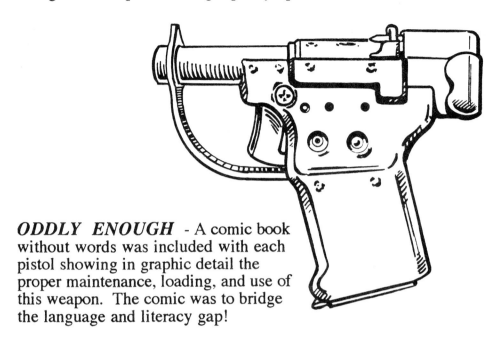

ODDLY ENOUGH - A comic book without words was included with each pistol showing in graphic detail the proper maintenance, loading, and use of this weapon. The comic was to bridge the language and literacy gap!

RUSS MILLER'S

ODDLY Enough©

The rather hideous Hagfish has fully developed eyes, but they are hidden under skin, making it completely blind. It has a rasping tongue, lined with teeth that it uses to tear holes in dead and dying fish on which it dines. The Hagfish literally eats the victims from the inside out, leaving only the skins.

ODDLY ENOUGH... When the Hagfish has difficulty gaining entry into the body of its meal, it does a very strange but effective thing. After locking its mouth onto the body of an animal, it throws a knot into its body and slides the knot down toward its head. Using the knot as leverage, it pulls its head through, and with it a chunk of the animal, usually leaving a hole large enough for the Hagfish to swim through!

Russ Miller's ODDLY Enough ©

King Henry VI, son of Frederick Barbarossa (1165-1197), had a rather direct approach to dealing with his enemies and conspirators. In 1197, Henry VI uncovered an assassination attempt that involved such high level individuals as the Pope (Celestine III) and Henry's estranged wife Constance of Sicily. Henry VI forced Constance to watch the executions of the various conspirators who were flayed alive, burned at the stake, covered in tar and ignited.

ODDLY ENOUGH - Constance was also forced to watch the execution of Jordanus o Sicily when a red-hot crown was affixed to his head with nails! (Henry VI also died the same year, of dysentery.)

Russ Miller's ODDLY Enough ©

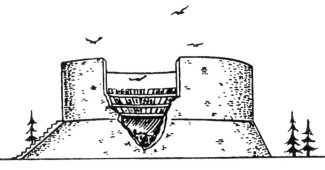

The Zoroastrians (a religious group primarily living in India and formerly of Persia) believe that one should never contaminate any of the natural elements: fire, water, earth, or air. Even in death, the bodies are not buried or burned, but rather taken to an open roof structure called a Dakhma ("tower of silence") to be rendered harmless to the earth.

ODDLY ENOUGH - Vultures reduce the bodies to bones in a very short period of time. Once the bones are clean and dry, they are placed in a pit at the center of the Dakhma, where they decompose to harmless dust, leaving no trace of their owners passing!

Stories of huge hailstones and monster sized snowflakes have been around for centuries. Some of them are most likely unreliable, however, there are enough verifiable stories to prove that such a phenomena does occur. A snow fall in Montana, January 28, 1887 reported snowflakes that measured 15 inches across and 8 inches thick. These "jumbo" flakes have been studied and we now know that they are clumps of many regular sized snowflakes. Giant hailstones have also been found to be globs of many stones crunched together. Still, there is no real explanation as to why this happens.

ODDLY ENOUGH - All of the shapes on this page reflect actual recorded hailstones! Some of these stones were quite large and many absolutely crystal clear!

Unusual objects have fallen from the skies throughout history. Many incidents absolutely defy explanation. For instance, there was a reported fall of hail in Columbia Missouri on November 11, 1911 that produced hailstones that exploded on impact! So loud were these "popping" hailstones that some people reported hearing gunshots. Other reports tell of huge hailstones falling so slowly that nothing that was struck was ever damaged. Another account tells of a hailstone that contained a chunk of alabaster inside.

ODDLY ENOUGH - A storm in Bovina (near Vicksburg Virginia) on May 11, 1894 produced a gopher turtle about 6 by 8 inches completely encased in a large stone of ice that fell during the storm!

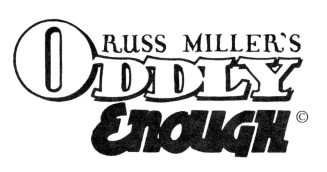

RUSS MILLER'S ODDLY ENOUGH ©

Elephants have been kept as domestic animals for thousands of years. Humans have trained them to do a variety of work including hauling loads, removing trees, and pulling vehicles. Some have even used elephants as living tanks during wartime. The typical life span of a domestic working elephant can be 70 to 80 years.

ODDLY ENOUGH - One of the strangest uses for elephants is that of executioner! Condemned criminals were once bound and dragged by pachyderms. If this punishing ordeal did not kill the person, the elephant was ordered to step on the criminal's head!

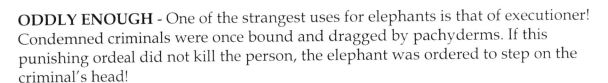

RUSS MILLER'S ODDLY ENOUGH ©

"Money" has taken many forms throughout history. In Thailand most parts of a tiger could be used as cash. In Burma, drums are considered valuable. Things such as dogs' teeth, whales' teeth, cowry shells, tea blocks, disc shaped stones, and bronze objects shaped like purchased goods have all been used at some time as currency.

ODDLY ENOUGH - The General Assembly of Virginia passed a law in 1642 declaring tobacco the only valid currency in the colony. Paper "tobacco notes" were issued to save people from having to carry large bundles of leaves with them. Talk about money to burn!

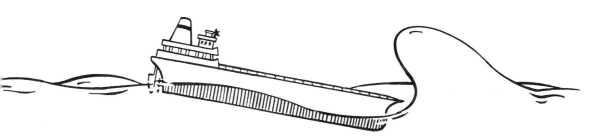

Freak, solitary waves of unusual height appear unpredictably, as though "out of nowhere", even mid-ocean and cannot be explained by wind or blowing storms. To label these freak waves as tidal waves is not accurate since they are probably caused by deep water seismic disturbances. These waves have been notorious in sinking or damaging ships at sea, as well as instantly sinking ships that were "securely" harbored. In 1881 such a wave struck a sailing ship called *ROSINA* in the North Atlantic and swept away everyone that was on deck at the time!

ODDLY ENOUGH - The same year, the *ROSINA* encountered another such wave. This time *everyone was on deck* shortening sail and, *everyone* was carried away except for one man who was ill and inside in his bunk! (He was eventually rescued by a passing steamer.)

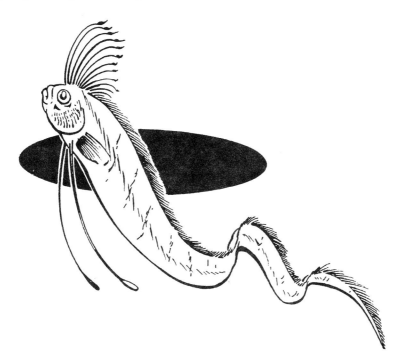

The Oar Fish, a silvery, ribbon-like fish with crimson markings, is extremely rare. It grows to more than 30 feet in length and has been known to weigh 600 pounds! It is called the "King of the Salmon" by Pacific Northwest Indians. It is believed that they feed on small crustaceans, but, unfortunately, very little is known of its biology.

ODDLY ENOUGH - It is assumed that many "sea serpent" sightings are due to the Oar Fish, since seeing a "red mane" (like the scarlet crest) is reported so often.

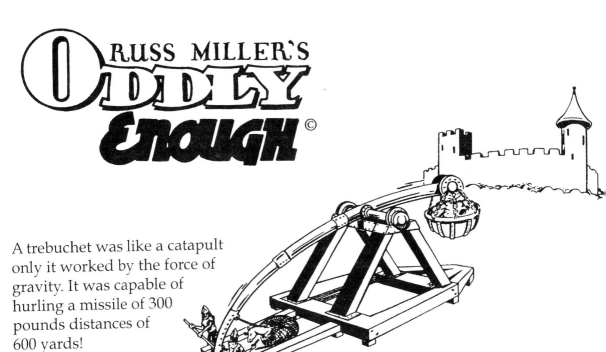

RUSS MILLER'S ODDLY Enough ©

A trebuchet was like a catapult only it worked by the force of gravity. It was capable of hurling a missile of 300 pounds distances of 600 yards!

ODDLY ENOUGH -
Trebuchets were often used to hurl putrefying animal carcasses over the walls of besieged towns in order to spread disease!

RUSS MILLER'S ODDLY Enough ©

It was a long believed by pirates that piercing of the ears and wearing earrings improved one's eyesight.

ODDLY ENOUGH - The point of the lobe where the ear was pierced corresponds to the auricular acupuncture point controlling the eyes!

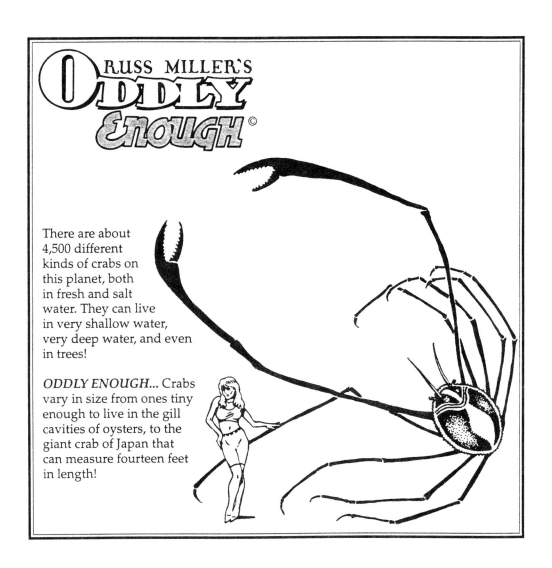

RUSS MILLER'S ODDLY ENOUGH ©

There are about 4,500 different kinds of crabs on this planet, both in fresh and salt water. They can live in very shallow water, very deep water, and even in trees!

ODDLY ENOUGH... Crabs vary in size from ones tiny enough to live in the gill cavities of oysters, to the giant crab of Japan that can measure fourteen feet in length!

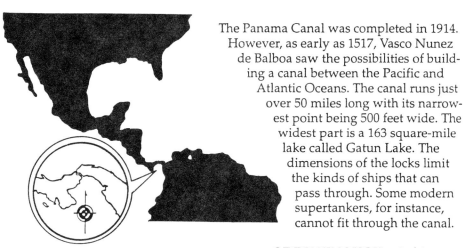

The Panama Canal was completed in 1914. However, as early as 1517, Vasco Nunez de Balboa saw the possibilities of building a canal between the Pacific and Atlantic Oceans. The canal runs just over 50 miles long with its narrowest point being 500 feet wide. The widest part is a 163 square-mile lake called Gatun Lake. The dimensions of the locks limit the kinds of ships that can pass through. Some modern supertankers, for instance, cannot fit through the canal.

ODDLY ENOUGH...A ship passing East to West, entering from the Atlantic Ocean ,will actually leave the canal (in the Pacific Ocean) 27 miles east of where it entered.

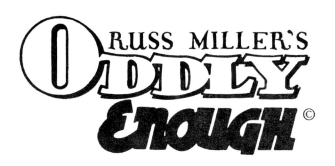

RUSS MILLER'S ODDLY ENOUGH ©

When Conquistador Hernando de Soto began his exploration of the New World, he carefully planned his expedition. Along with his men, horses, equipment, and dogs, de Soto also included some "starvation insurance" in the form of 13 Spanish hogs that he hoped would procreate along the way. The hogs also probably protected the men against poisonous snakes since hogs actively hunt and kill reptiles. The herd, however, became quite a nuisance when their numbers began to grow, and de Soto refused to butcher them, fearing that survival might become even more extreme further into the frontier. De Soto demanded that his men eat dogs before sacrificing the pigs.

ODDLY ENOUGH - By the time of his death in 1542, having found no treasure and having traversed some 4,000 miles, the "pampered pigs" numbered 700! Shortly after interring his body in the Mississippi river Hernando de Soto's men auctioned off the hogs and ate their fill of roast pork.

RUSS MILLER'S ODDLY ENOUGH ©

Wigs have been used for thousands of years by a variety of cultures. Many societies actually chose to shave their heads so that they could wear intricately fashioned wigs. The Egyptians braided human hair with plant fiber and beeswax. In eighteenth century England, wigs were greased and powdered with flour, starch and gold dust. In some cases, wigs have been known to be so large and heavy that the wearer needed assistance in order to walk with it on his head.

ODDLY ENOUGH - A Greek theologian named Clement suggested that priests could not adequately bless a wig wearer, because the blessing would remain on top of the wig and not descend through it to the wearer. By 692 AD, Christian wig wearers could be excommunicated!

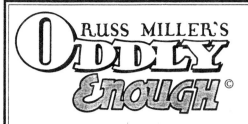

RUSS MILLER'S ODDLY Enough©

The largest flower known to man is found in Indonesia and is called *Rafflesia arnoldii*. It has no roots and no green photosynthetic material, yet it measures more than forty inches across and can weigh in excess of fifteen pounds!

ODDLY ENOUGH ... This flower is not pollinated by bees, but rather its pollen is carried by flies that are attracted to its fetid odor. Sometimes called the "stinking corpse lily," the huge *Rafflesia arnoldii* smells like rotting flesh!

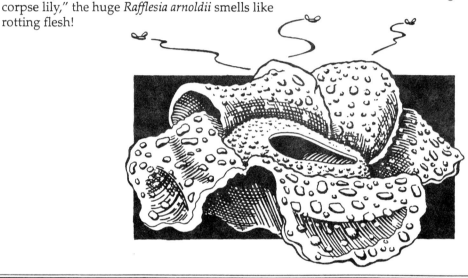

Scientists rank bamboo as one of the most primitive grasses on this planet. Some bamboo has been known to grow to a height of 120 feet with a stem one foot in diameter. This strange plant rarely blooms, and usually dies soon after. It has been used to build houses, make furniture, sandals, rope, paper, cages, fishing poles, even reinforce concrete. The young shoots can also be eaten as vegetables.

ODDLY ENOUGH ... Bamboo is probably the fastest growing plant we know of, in one instance growing an unbelievable 36 inches in 24 hours'

RUSS MILLER'S ODDLY Enough ©

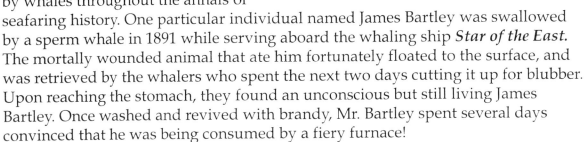

The story of Jonah may not be as fanciful as it first appears. There have been several accounts of men being gulped by whales throughout the annals of seafaring history. One particular individual named James Bartley was swallowed by a sperm whale in 1891 while serving aboard the whaling ship *Star of the East.* The mortally wounded animal that ate him fortunately floated to the surface, and was retrieved by the whalers who spent the next two days cutting it up for blubber. Upon reaching the stomach, they found an unconscious but still living James Bartley. Once washed and revived with brandy, Mr. Bartley spent several days convinced that he was being consumed by a fiery furnace!

ODDLY ENOUGH - James Bartley later wrote of his horrific experience and recalled that the worst part of the ordeal was the relentless darkness, and the terrific heat inside the whale's body. Mr. Bartley recounted that his comprehension was completely clear and sharp up until the time he passed out!

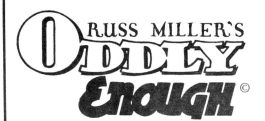

RUSS MILLER'S ODDLY Enough ©

Although the giraffe has a neck seven feet long, it contains the same number of vertebrae as that of a mouse - seven. The giraffe, like the cow, chews its cud and can run faster than a horse. Giraffes can completely seal their nostrils at will against dust and wind, and although they do have a voice, it is seldom heard and it is very soft.

ODDLY ENOUGH - The first giraffe ever seen in the West was brought to Rome about 46 BC by Julius Caesar!

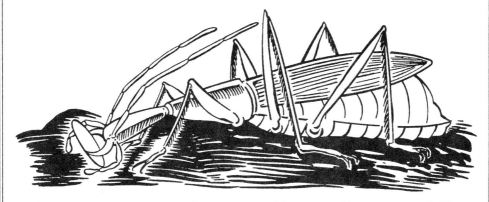

RUSS MILLER'S ODDLY Enough ©

Beetles are one of the largest and most successful groups of insects on earth. They are wonderfully diverse and have developed remarkable specialties within their ranks. One of the most specialized is the quarter-inch-long rhadinid beetle. It is a blind, cave dwelling insect that lives almost exclusively on the buried eggs of crickets. Using its head like a hoe, it excavates the eggs and sucks them dry, leaving only the shriveled bags of membrane behind.

ODDLY ENOUGH...the rhadinid beetle, like a prospector, finds the eggs hidden in the silt of the cave floor using specialized sensory organs. These sensors pick up chemical substances left by the cricket. This technique, combined with detection of minute irregularities on the surface, show the beetle where to dig!

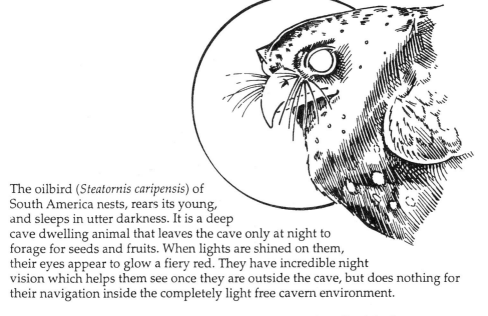

The oilbird (*Steatornis caripensis*) of South America nests, rears its young, and sleeps in utter darkness. It is a deep cave dwelling animal that leaves the cave only at night to forage for seeds and fruits. When lights are shined on them, their eyes appear to glow a fiery red. They have incredible night vision which helps them see once they are outside the cave, but does nothing for their navigation inside the completely light free cavern environment.

ODDLY ENOUGH... In the evening when all is quiet, the oilbird finds its way through the darkness by creating a din of noise produced by a steady stream of clicks which echo off the cave walls and subterranean structures. In spite of its three foot wingspan, oilbirds can maneuver in total darkness!

RUSS MILLER'S ODDLY Enough©

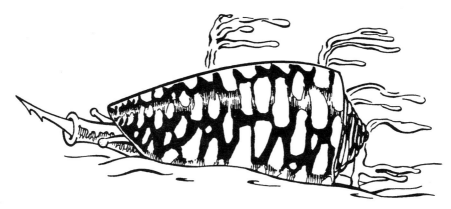

The Cone Shell Mollusk (of which there are hundreds of types) is a snail that can actually fish for its dinner! Using a tonguelike organ that contains a poison "harpoon," the Cone Shell spears its victim with blinding speed. Tough ligaments hold the barbed harpoon fast to the Cone Shell as it "reels in" its prey. So potent is the venom of this little animal that some can kill humans in a few minutes. Some Cone Shell Mollusk shells sell for thousands of dollars to collectors.

ODDLY ENOUGH... The Cone Shell Mollusk is blind. It senses its prey by "tasting" the water while hiding in rocks or sand!

The Sea Snake (a member of the Cobra Family of which their are 50 to 60 species) can grow to the length of 9 feet. Their bodies are flattened sideways allowing them to swim with great skill. Sea Snakes can spend as much as eight hours underwater without taking a breath.

They have been known to amass by the millions during breeding season, and cause a serious hazard to fishermen who bring them up by the hundreds in their nets. A bite from some snakes can bring death to an adult in minutes.

ODDLY ENOUGH... Many fish won't eat Sea Snakes even though their flesh is not toxic because these snakes will bite a fish from the inside, killing it instantly, and then swim back out the mouth!

The octopus is a remarkable animal with a highly developed brain, and extremely good eye sight. Possessing superb defenses they can rapidly change color, squirt a cloud of ink (that smells like octopus to many predators), and even grow new limbs when attacked. Large octopuses can measure close to 30 feet from tentacle tip to tentacle tip. The tiny Blue-Ringed octopus is one of the deadliest creatures in the ocean. It can inject its victims with a large dose of TTX, a poison also found in the Death Puffer fish.

ODDLY ENOUGH - The Blue-Ringed octopus is so poisonous that it can kill without even biting its victim. It can merely release its venom into the water near its prey, and the victim will die after pumping the poisonous water through its gills!

Elvis Presley was told by a music teacher that he showed little promise as a musician. The talent manager of the Grand Ole Opry in Nashville told him he should consider a career driving a truck. He went on to earn 4 million dollars a year as a performer.

The Mona Lisa, painted by Leonardo da Vinci once hung in the bathroom of Francis I, King of France.

Until the 15th century diamonds were predominantly worn by men.

Mongolian armies, when they wished to travel fast, would puncture a vein of their horse, and drink about a half a pint of blood. This way they didn't need to stop and cook a meal.

240'

Roman emperor Caligula was as ostentatious as he was insane. He once commissioned two private barges to be built for his decadent pleasure. These huge boats were said to be fitted with baths, galleries, bars, carved marble work, and even living trees and assorted plants growing on board! Years later, the barges fell into disrepair and sank to the bottom of Lake Nemi, just outside of Rome, Italy. In 1928, Benito Mussolini drained Lake Nemi to expose the two large, ancient vessels. Some of the marble columns and statues were found within the remaining hulls.

ODDLY ENOUGH - Whatever was left of these two magnificent ships was completely burned in 1944 by the retreating German Army!

A Russian man by the name of Chamouni was a celebrity labeled "Salamander" because of his peculiar act. Billed as "The Incombustible", Chamouni would enter a large oven with a raw leg of mutton, and later emerge after the leg was well baked. It is believed that the ovens would achieve temperatures of 250 degrees or higher.

ODDLY ENOUGH - The famous "Russian Salamander" was cremated after he died performing his stunt!

Russ Miller's ODDLY Enough ©

Known affectionately as "The Wizard of Menlo Park", Thomas Alva Edison invented many of the devices that we take for granted today. Most people know that Thomas Edison invented the incandescent lamp, but fewer know that he invented motion pictures as we know them, the phonograph, the microphone, the chemical phenol, the electric vote recorder, the radio vacuum tube, and the carbon telephone transmitter. Thomas Edison also published a newspaper called the *Weekly Herald* when he was fifteen in order to make money to fund his experiments.

ODDLY ENOUGH - Thomas Edison was also the inventor of waxed paper!

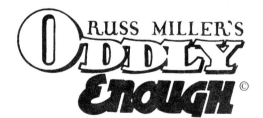

Russ Miller's ODDLY Enough ©

Fossils can range from the size of one-celled animals to mastodons and be preserved as petrified objects, molds (cavities), prints, or whole animals and plants. During the Middle Ages in Europe, many naturalists thought fossils were produced by a mysterious "plastic force" that formed fossils in the Earth. People even hired sculptors to "manufacture" fossils from time to time.

ODDLY ENOUGH - During the 1720's, a scientist named Joham Beringer unearthed some phony fossils (including grapes) that had been deliberately carved and placed where he could find them. Beringer published his findings and was completely humiliated when the truth was revealed.

RUSS MILLER'S ODDLY Enough ©

Millions of years ago, in the ancient waters of the earth, strange fish swam, including such bony fishes as this Gorgonichthys. This bony plated placoderm is believed to have been a predator and reached lengths of over 20 feet. Heavy armored fish like this one have been discovered in fossils found in North America, Morocco, China, Latvia, and Australia.

ODDLY ENOUGH... Some of these bony plated fish even had bones in their eyes!

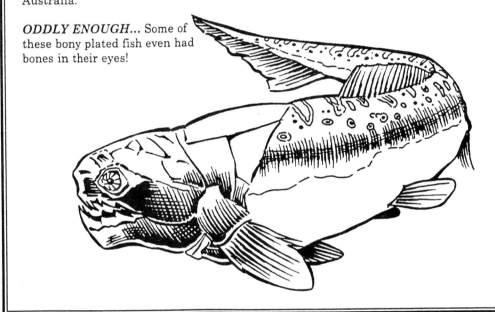

Scorpions vary in size from an inch to 8 inches in length.
All scorpions bear their young live. These arachnids (not insects) are excellent hunters with 6 to 8 eyes, two pairs of pincers, and startling speed. Hunting usually at night, they feed on spiders, insects, and small animals.

ODDLY ENOUGH... Putting a tiny amount of liquor on a scorpion will cause it to immediately go mad and sting itself to death!

When frogs hibernate, they stop breathing as they normally do, and instead take in air through their skin. Frogs can be found throughout the world and in a variety of shapes and sizes. Some frogs are used by Aboriginal people to poison the tips of their arrows. One frog of Asia has feet so big, it can actually glide from tree to tree. A tropical frog in central Africa, when full grown, is no larger than a housefly.

ODDLY ENOUGH... The Giant Frog of Africa measures two and a half feet long and weighs more than 14 pounds! That's larger and heavier than a standard mason's cinder building block.

RUSS MILLER'S ODDLY Enough ©

The fossil record of sharks is a curious and intriguing one. Some shark remains show the presence of a brushlike structure, bristling with teeth, perched on top of dorsal fins. Scientists have no idea what its function was. One of the most bizarre-looking of these prehistoric fish is the Helicoprion shark which sported a strange whorl of teeth. Some believe this coil at the front of the lower jaw was used to thrash through schools of squid or fish in order to stun them.

ODDLY ENOUGH... though peculiar, this type of shark was highly successful, spreading around the world during the Permian Period and being found in North America, Russia, Japan, and Australia!

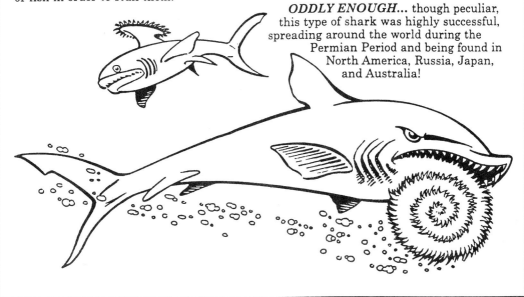

The Odd Creator of Oddly Enough

It's easy to see that odd and unusual facts are a passion with Russ Miller when you realize that at the age of eight he read himself to sleep every night with his encyclopedia, starting with **A** and working his way relentlessly to **Z**. The quest for academic excellence was with him when in grade school he wrote a 12 page paper on insects and presented it in class. "Um, that will be quite enough, young man," Mrs. Caldwell murmured unappreciatively after the third page of his oral presentation, "You may sit down now."

Never daunted, through the years Russ has continued to consider research and academic excellence to be of paramount importance. He was well into his courses in pre-med at Arizona State University, when a new passion overtook him. **Art**. No one was more surprised than he (except maybe his parents) when midway through his Bachelors Degree program, a sudden sense of knowing where he belonged caused him to change his major to drawing and painting. Perhaps it wasn't all that surprising considering his youthful enthusiasm for building and painting model airplanes, accurate in every detail, of course. Russ received his bachelors degree in fine art and drawing from ASU in 1975.

It was a different kind of passion that brought him to Fuller Theological Seminary in Pasadena, California in the Fall of 1976. He wanted to unite his background in art with his growing faith in God and his church involvement. As always, academic excellence was the first order of the day. In the course of a two year Master of Arts degree program he met and married his wife, Janice. "We worked across the hall from each other. He was the typical starving artist, or at least it seemed so to me. I liked to offer him tidbits of things to eat. One thing led to another and soon I was cooking all his meals." Russ and Janice have two children, Kristin 13, and Erik 9... plus a small menagerie.

"Well.. what now?" was the blunt question posed by friends and family after his graduation from Fuller in 1979. More school was the last response they were expecting to hear, but that was the plan. He entered the Master of Fine Arts program with an emphasis in sculpture at California State University, L.A. Over the next two years he created a myriad of pieces of sculpture uniting his love of highly polished wood, brass, found objects (a lovely, romantic walk could quickly turn into a scavengers hunt through trash cans), and social commentary. "All your pieces have stories behind them," one of his classmates once commented. Never satisfied with simply creating objects of beauty, he was always looking for a deeper meaning, considering the role of the artist as a commentator on all that he saw happening around him. His Masters show culminated two years of creativity.

R. Miller in Flight traced the development of the airplane from the joyful adventure of the early days to a machine of destruction in a succession of wars. As always, there was a story to tell. *Oddly Enough,* after this one man show which featured a piece dedicated to Amelia Earhart, Russ found out that he was related to her!

Through the last two decades Russ Miller has freelanced for companies as diverse as DuPont, Caterpillar Machinery, H&K Firearms and World Vision. His writing, art, and humor have been featured in many national and international publications including: Disney, Marvel, Eclipse, Now Comics, Edge Publishing, Gladstone, Another Rainbow, The New Times, Gauntlet, Action Planet, Press, and Rage. He is also a part time instructor at a local college teaching Comparative Religions, and Commercial Art.

Oddly Enough has been an ongoing passion uniting both his talent for unearthing unusual facts and his abilities as an artist. Syndicated by Singer Media in 1995, and distributed throughout Europe, each feature contains a nugget of strange information, always with that "Oddly Enough" twist at the end. "This is a project I could never get bored producing," Miller states confidently. And when you consider how long he has been pursuing this interest, I think it's fairly likely he is right.